UNDERWEAR Do's and Don'ts

Todd Parr

Megan Tingley Books
LITTLE, BROWN AND COMPANY
New York Boston

Little, Brown and Company

Time Warner Book Group
1271 Avenue of the Americas, New York, NY 10020
Visit our Web site at www.lb-kids.com

First 9x9 Edition: February 2005

Library of Congress Cataloging-in-Publication Data

Parr, Todd.
    Underwear do's and don'ts / Todd Parr. — 1st ed.
        p.   cm.
    ISBN 0-316-69151-8 (hc)/ISBN 0-316-90806-1 (bb)/ISBN 0-316-05964-1 (hc 9x9)
    1. Underwear — Humor. I. Title.
PN6231.U52 P37 2000
818'.5402 — dc21   99-052647

10 9 8 7 6 5 4 3 2 1

PHX

Printed in the United States of America

For my Dad for always
making me laugh.
Love,
Todd

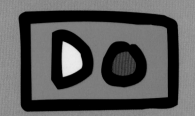

Have lots of different kinds of underwear

Don't

Wear it all at once

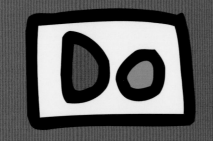

Wash your underwear

DO

Put your clean underwear away

Put it in the freezer

DO

Wear underwear to the beach

Do

Go shopping for
underwear with a hippo

Don't

Let her try it on

RRIP

Dress up your dog in underwear

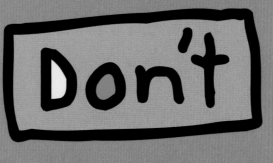

Don't

Use your sister's favorite pair

DO

Wear fancy underwear under your dress

Don't

Hang upside down on the monkey bars

Do

Give cool underwear
as a present

Go swimming in
your underwear

Don't

Jump off the diving board

Do

Wear polka-dot underwear to a party

Don't

Wear a plain pair

Do

Wear striped underwear if you're a zebra

Don't

Wear polka-dotted ones

Do

Bring extra underwear
when you go fishing

No matter what underwear you wear, always feel good about yourself!

Love,
Todd